MO KANE

A Ruben Kane Novel

By

EDDIE J MARTIN

Thanks to Barbara A. Martin (my wife) for her help on editing this novel.

CONTENTS

THE LETTER

I WAS SITTING at my desk, nursing a cup of java when Rita came in with the morning paper, mail, which included the usual bills—gas, water, electric, and a letter postmarked Alaska, but no forwarding address. I opened it and the first thing I pulled out was a picture of Smooth and his girls—four of them. I was sure there used to be five. The letter was a page and a half and it read something like this:

RK,

I know you're surprised to hear from me but guess who? Since I last wrote you, 5 years ago from Mexico, I've traveled around the world, especially to areas where there are no wars. I even bought myself an island, until I got run off by the Japanese. Holland is still cool and we lived there for a little while. We also went to Paris after the Germans got kicked out. We also checked out and made a move to Hawaii because of the weather. We stayed there for a couple of years. Now we've settled down in Alaska of all places.

You won't believe what pussy is selling for up here. RK, it's at least fifty men to every one woman; and I came up here with five. I came with a gold mine, do you hear me RK, a gold mine. Give me five years and I'll be running this mother.

6   *Mo Kane*

Got me five more girls, one of my original five got married on me. Get this, she married the mayor of the town—ain't that some shit? She still comes by every now and then to see old Smooth and give me some of that honey. That brings me to why I'm writing you.

There is this lady that's coming down your way and she'll be needing your help. I don't know all the particulars but I'm sure you'll do your best, besides it's right down your alley! You're gonna thank me for this one, RK. This lady is something special, I told her all about you and that you were my main man. She'll call you when she arrives; knowing her she'll be staying at the best hotel in town. By the way, her name is Willow; Janice Willow.

Smooth was a local pimp around here, who when the war came along, felt he didn't want to serve, so he decided to make a run for the southern border. Uncle Sam's boys looked for him but never found him. After a while, they stopped looking. He wrote when he

first took off but that was five years ago. The war was getting hot and heavy by then. I never heard from Smooth again until now. Smooth's mother passed away while he was on the run but since he couldn't be reached, he never knew. I wanted to write him and tell him the bad news. I know he's gonna take it bad because he and his mom were real close. Since it was two years ago, I took it on myself to handle the funeral arrangements. All the girls he walked the streets with were there, and Smooth's mother had been a prostitute. Her friend from New Orleans came up, and her daughter she had sent up here a few years earlier was there. All in all, it was a pretty decent crowd. Smooth would have been proud.

Okay, there he goes again. He left here 5 years ago in some shit, but now he's back by way of some chick to screw my life up again. I wonder what it is this time.

I'll bet anything it will be hell getting my money

from her, unless they think I'm giving out charity.

Smooth knows I don't play that!

2

RITA

"RITA, WOULD YOU please bring me another cup of

coffee?" Rita is my secretary, who has been with me for

several years. She is of Mexican descent and is in the

country illegally.

I've been trying to get her papers to sponsor her, and

she has been going to school to better her English.

She's 5 foot 4, and 250 pounds, with long black hair and large pretty black eyes.

She has a tattoo on her left shoulder and has a blade, can't forget the stiletto she carries in her bra—there's plenty of room to hide it there. At least one guy found out the hard way about that blade.

Rita brought in the coffee and breakfast. "Do you want a breakfast burrito?"

No, thank you. I took out my bottle of Jim Bean and poured two fingers into my coffee cup. Some might say I'm an alcoholic. It may be true, but I always loved coffee with my Bean. Regardless—I'm never without a drink. The day doesn't seem to go right without that first drink. And who knows? I may stop drinking right after this next one. For a man that's been in this business for many years now, with a wife and a girlfriend. My wife, Ella and I—well, we just live together. Why we live together is a mystery to me, and it shouldn't be because I am a detective.

Sometimes I would ask myself where the love went. Most of the time I'm with Freda, my girlfriend, who has everything that the wife doesn't and who does the things the wife doesn't. But there is a reason I won't move in with her even though I have been asked—I just don't know it yet. Between my work and my two ladies, plus the ones I meet on my cases, I don't have any time left. You would think a man my size and age—44-years-old, 5'8 and 180 pounds—wouldn't be able to move like I do, but I get around. With my tweed sport coat, black fedora, grey wool pants and black old man comforts, "Stetson shoes" I'm a typical private detective. All I need now is a client. I don't know when this woman that Smooth is sending is going to show up, but I hope she's a paying customer.

"RK, Bernie is on line one."

"Hey Bernie, what's up? You forgot that little change you owe us, didn't you, RK? You know we don't do business like that. When can I expect

payment?"

Bernie is the local bookie, we are so close that sometimes, I can even get my bets on credit. For a short time, anyway. Believe it or not, I just forgot Bernie don't play that, or his employers don't.

"Bernie, I'll get your money to you, don't worry about it."

"Oh, I'm not worried, RK. The people I work for kind of are; but I'm not worried. It doesn't matter if we are friends."

"Okay, okay, Bernie. I'll get it to you as soon as possible. In the meantime, put $2 each on 256, 748 and 931 for me. And put $20 on shoelace to show."

Rita called out, "Raymond is on the line."

"Thanks, Rita. Raymond, what's up, dude?

How are you sitting for employment these days RK?"

"I just finished a case the other day, so my case load is pretty much clear as of today, but I'm waiting for a client that should be here in the next few days. But let's hear what you got."

Raymond is a barber that's been around for over 30 years, he knows everything that's going on in town and spreads it around for a fee.

From time to time he contacts me after someone has contacted him, looking to hire someone in my profession and the work I do.

"It's like this, RK. There is this guy who suspects his wife is cheating on him, and he wants to divorce her. But he wants to do that without paying support.

He needs to get the goods on her. He asked if I knew anyone who could help him with that and right away, I thought of you."

"I want to thank you for thinking of me, Raymond, but I think I'll pass on this one."

"You sure, RK? It pays well!"

"Yeah, I'm sure Raymond, but keep me in mind for the next one."

After Raymond hung up, RK thought, *Oh hell no, I'm not taking anything like that again. The last time I took a case like that, the husband ended up in the hospital, the wife was put in jail for six months, and my license was suspended for a year. Besides that, I didn't get paid. No! I'll pass on this one and any others after this.*

At one o'clock, I decided to head for lunch at that Skippy's—a diner I normally go for its pig feet, pig ears, and pig tails—stone soul food. You can't find it anywhere else in town. It's not a large place but the food is excellent. On the way there, I needed to stop by the service station to gas up my 1938 Buick. It seems gas is getting higher and higher.

At $.28 a gallon, its way too high. They're going to have to do something about that. It took the attendant ten minutes to service my tires, wash my windshield, and put the gas, oil, and water in. These old boys are getting slow. I may have to find myself another service station, especially at these prices.

After lunch I stopped off at the house I share with Ella, my wife. Sometimes, I get calls there and Ella neglects to call me and inform me about them. I wonder why! I walked in the door of the 2nd floor apartment and there was Ella, folding clothes. I noticed they were all hers—I didn't even see a pair of my drawls. But that's power for the course.

"Well, look what the wind blew in, you lost Ruben?"

"No Ella, I'm just stopping by to see if I had any messages. Are there any?"

"No, there are not, Ruben. The ones that did call I referred them to your office."

"Well, thank you for that, Ella."

I walked into my room, changed out my clothes and took a shower. I changed my shirt, pants and socks. I walked back into the room where Ella was, looked in the kitchen cabinet, and brought out my bottle of Jim Bean.

"You never forget where that is, do you?"

"And how have you been doing, Ella? You sitting here in this kitchen still hating the world?"

"After being away from home for a week now, how the hell would you know who I'm hating on? I could have a man laying up in here right now and you'd never know or care."

"Do you really want to go down this road, Ella? After all, you've got your affairs and I know it, so what do you want to do? I've asked you several times about splitting up but you don't seem to want to do that—something about religion, I guess, I don't know."

"Look, Ruben. The way I feel about it, we're just roommates anyway, and it's cheaper for both of us to live this way, so let's let it be."

"Well, Ella. It was nice having this conversation, we must do it again sometime."

"You didn't forget to pay the rent, did you?"

"No, I didn't. Did you forget to pay the utilities?"

"Everything except the water, you can pay that."

Since there was nothing else on my agenda, I decided to head for the office.

When I stopped at the light, a fine young thing was

crossing the street. My eyes followed her from the time

she stepped off the curb until she was on the other side.

She had high heels, a short skirt that was way above

the knees, and see-through halter on. She wore

earrings with little clowns hanging down—one

laughing and one crying. She didn't have any lipstick

on, but lips like that didn't need any.

   She had an hour glass waist and hips. Oh, my Lord!

When she passed by me, she turned her head and

looked at me, perked her lips in a kiss and winked. I

put the Buick in neutral and the hand brakes on, got

out and just stared after her. I watched that ass doing

the 'come get it' thing. I had thoughts of doing just that

when the vehicles behind me started honking their

horns and given me the finger. Next time, Ms. Lady,

next time.

3

MEETING WILLOW

"DID YOU HAVE a nice lunch?" Rita asked.

"I did, any calls?"

"Yes, there was one. You received a call from a Miss Janice Willow. She said Smooth referred her. She left her number; it's at the Commodore Hotel."

"Miss Willow, Ruben Kane speaking. When did you get in?"

"Oh, I flew in late last night."

"I didn't receive the letter from Smooth until

today, he must have send it on a slow boat. How about I pick you up tonight for dinner and cocktails, say about seven?"

"That'll be fine, Mr. Kane. I'm in room 1215. Give me a call from the lobby and I'll come down."

"See you then, Miss Willow!"

The old girl sounded pretty good, Ruben thought. But when I meet her, first thing's first—the money! Depending on what I can help her with. Smooth knows the kind of work I do, he should have told her, and I'm sure he did. Smooth was right about one thing, that high dollar hotel she's staying in—that's the most expensive in town. I guess when I take her out to dinner it can't be to a hole in the wall. The Rooster-tail should do it. It's a top-notch restaurant, the drinks are top of the line, there is a nice combo with piano, bass and drums, and the riff raff stays out—it's too expensive! I'm gonna have to hit my savings for this one, but I guess no deposit, no return.

I guess it would be out of order to ask her to pay. That goddamn Smooth! Glad I took a shower and changed clothes. I' am ready to go now. Rita had told me she was leaving about an hour ago. I took a hit of JB and laid down on the couch.

Two hours later, I was headed for the Commodore Hotel. I walked into the lobby and over to the house phone and dialed Room 1215. Willow picked up the phone and said, "Yes?"

"Miss Willow, this is Ruben Kane. I' am down in the lobby."

"Come on up, Mr. Kane."

What the hell? he thought. She said she was coming down, but she must have forgot. Oh, well!

I wasn't ready for the lady that opened the door; 5 foot 11 without heels and 3 inches taller than me. I would have guessed she was about a hundred and 50 pounds, with almond skin. She looked more like an Indian than a colored woman. She had a long straight nose, and a wide mouth with kissable lips. Her eyes were large and wide, and her eyebrows were trimmed and thin. Her hair was reddish-brown and wavy, and was cut into a boyish bob. Her fingers were long and slender. She wore a black pants suit with a two-inch belt around the waist. Miss Willow looked like an athlete of the future and I knew right then that I was in love.

"Come in Mr. Kane, come in!" She grabbed me by my jacket, pulled me into the apartment and closed the door behind me.

"What the?"

"Come with me," she said. I followed her into the bedroom and there on the floor was a man, about 42 years old laying on his stomach with a knife sticking out of the back of his neck. The furniture was displaced all over the room, and bags were opened and their contents thrown all over the bed. The clothes drawers were pulled out and the clothes in the closet were thrown out. He had a 45 automatic in his outstretched hand.

"What the hell happened here?"

"When I came out of the bathroom, that's who I found searching my room."

"How the hell did he get in here?"

"I think he came over from the adjoining apartment, through the balcony area. I looked and you can step from one apartment to the other. To make a long story short," she said, "he tried to kill me."

"Well, I can see it didn't work out too good for him." I leaned down and checked him for a pulse. He was dead as an Alaskan salmon.

"How long will it take to clean this mess?" she asked.

"Me?" I said. "What the hell have I to do with this? I just got here."

"Look, Mr. Kane. Smooth told me you were cool and you know how to handle things like this, is there going to be a problem?"

"Hold on! Hold on! Let me think for a minute. You want to explain what's going on here? Who the hell are you?"

"You can call me Janice, and I'll tell you what, I'll call you Ruben. Now, I'll tell you everything at dinner, I promise. In the meantime, you'll do what you do. Make your calls or whatever, and get this place cleaned up. I'll be in the other room having a drink."

THE ROOSTER TAIL

"THE ROOSTER TAIL, Janice said. is that what they call it? I like it." The club was by the river and had a patio with about 20 tables and chairs, a bar with thirty stools or more, and maybe twenty-five dinner tables inside, with a three-piece jazz combo. This was one of the few clubs in town that was totally integrated.

"Yeah, it's alright. Our table won't be ready for another thirty minutes, so let's go over to the bar."

At the bar, Janice ordered a gin and tonic and Ruben ordered his favorite, Jim Bean on the rocks.

"What time is my apartment going to be ready?" Janice asked

"It'll be clean by the time we get bac."

"Are you still mad at me Ruben? Don't be mad, honey. I was just trying to protect myself," she said as she reached over and patted his hand.

Ruben looked at her, and kind of melted. Damn, she's one fine mother jumper.

"Smooth told me you knew what to do when things turned south. He also said that you're all about the dollar bill. I'm sure you'll like what I'm going to offer you."

She took a pen out of her purse and picked up a napkin off the bar and wrote a number on it, then slid it over to Ruben for him to see.

Ruben looked at it, took a drink and said, "What do I have to do for this?" He didn't let on how impressed he was. "You know, everything costs money around here, even that clean-up job I had done."

"I need someone to watch my back." Janice took the paper back and wrote another number, then passed it to Ruben again. It was twice what it was the first time. At that point, Ruben said, "You want to tell me what I'm in for?"

"Four men robbed a home in a very exclusive part of town in California. They got in the safe and retrieved something they shouldn't have. The people that hired me want it back. The guy, back there in my room, was one of the four guys in on the robbery."

"How and when did you run into Smooth?"

"I followed them up from Los Angeles to Portland, Oregon, then to Seattle, Washington, and onto Anchorage, Alaska. That's where I ran into a little trouble and Smooth helped me out. I found out that they were headed to Cleveland, and Smooth happened to mention he was from there; and he knew you."

"What are these guys doing here in Cleveland?" Ruben asked.

"What they do wherever they go, rob people!"

"How did you happen to get hired? It's kind of unusual for a woman to get a job like this."

"What can I say, Ruben, except that I'm good at what I do."

"One more thing, Janice. What are you going to do when you catch up to them?"

"What do you mean, Ruben? I'm going to get my client's property back and hope to come out of it in one piece."

"What I mean is, they are not all going to end up like our friend back there in the room, are they?" Ruben said.

"Well, I can't say, Ruben, that's up to them."

The waiter came over to them at the bar and told them that their table was ready.

REGGIE

AFTER JANICE AND Ruben returned to the hotel room, they looked around the bedroom, bathroom, closet, under the bed, and behind the couch. They didn't find a thing out of place, and the clothes were back in the closet and drawers. The bags were on the bed and the clothes were folded where they were supposed to be. The lamps were picked up and the bed was made. The most important thing was that there was no dead body and no trace of blood anywhere. The 45 that belonged to the intruder was also gone.

Janice looked through her bags. At the bottom left-hand corner in a false bottom was a small 22 automatic pistol, a silencer and two clips of ammunition.

"Yes, Ruben, your people do good work."

"I had a good teacher."

"The knife, I seem to remember a knife." Did they take that too?"

"No, I retrieved that before we went to dinner. You think that was a good idea?"

"I'm sure of it," Janice replied.

After Ruben did another walk-through of the apartment, he told Janice he'd check back with her around 11 a.m. the next morning. Ruben had to make a few phone calls to see who was new in town and they would go from there.

"That's cool, I have to make a few calls myself."

"Raymond, this is Ruben. I need to pick your brain about something."

"RK, I didn't think you'd get back to me so soon. Did you change your mind about the job?"

"No, I haven't changed my mind but, I may be able to lay a few dollars on you if you can help me."

"If I can help you? Well, I don't know, RK. The

person who called me could use your help, and was depending on me to talk to you. Plus, he laid a few coins on me up front, so you can see how it is, RK. I kind of owe the guy."

"I see, is that the way it's gonna be, Raymond?" Is that the way you gonna play your old buddy?"

"I got no choice RK, I'm hurting here. Now, if you just give me your word, you'd look into that little matter I asked you about. Maybe we could help each other out."

"OK, Raymond. How about this; you tell me what you can on my case, and I'll see what I can do to help you."

"Deal. Oh, and I still expect to get paid on whatever I can help you with."

After asking Raymond the usual questions, strangers in town, rumors of a heist going down, and high dollar stuff up for sale, he informed me that he hadn't heard of anything yet, but you never can tell who came into the shop with what. Then, I asked Raymond if he heard of a woman that was in town in the same line of work I was in—an investigator.

"Hell no. I sure enough would have heard about her. I'll tell you who would know, your old buddy Reggie out of Chicago. You remember Reggie, don't you? (Long Pause) RK, RK? Are you there?"

"Yeah, I'm here Raymond... And yes, I remember Reggie. What would he know about what goes on here in Cleveland? Those old boys know everything, and they sure know what goes on in their industry. I'll bet he can call her up for you in two seconds."

"Thanks, Raymond, but I was hoping I wouldn't be seeing or talking to Reggie for a while—like never!"

Reggie was a hitman of the highest caliber. He didn't just kill a mark, he killed a mark. If he likes you, he shoots you between the eyes—hc calls that doing you a favor. If he doesn't like you, then he takes a straight razor to you. I don't even like thinking about it. I was hired by him through Raymond to find his daughter, who one of our local pimps conned into coming over here and it turned out to be a prostitution ring for young girls. I found out where they were and Reggie felt I needed help collecting them, so he came over to give me a hand. They would have done better dealing with me. Five men and one woman ended up dead, and two of the men had their penis cut off, and all other unspeakable things that I tried to forget.

The woman (the boss) I heard was on a cruise when he caught up with her and she was lost at sea. Reggie is no one to play with, but I will say we departed on good terms. Raymond may be right,

Reggie may be able to tell me something

about Janice. At least now I will be going into this with my eyes wide open, or partly open, anyway. Reggie had left me with his card of where to contact him if need be. If he wasn't there they know where to find him. The number I called in Chicago had an extension, and two minutes later, Reggie was on the line.

"Ruben, how you doing? This is a surprise. What do I owe the pleasure of this call?"

"Well, Reggie, it has to do with business or I wouldn't bother you, although it is good talking to you again. How long has it been, a year, two? I need to ask you something that I'm thinking only you would know about. At least no one seems to know around here in Cleveland."

"I'll try, Ruben. What is it?"

"I recently got hired by this young lady from the West Coast, black, 5 foot 11, athletic-looking and beautiful. Looks like an Indian or Creole. As soon as I met her, she was in some shit and pulled me right along, so much so that I had to call your people… to help me out."

"Yes, I know. I heard about it."

"You did? I'm surprised!"

"You should know by now, Ruben, that nothing gets past us when it comes to "that". Now, what is it you want to know?"

1. Who is she?

2. What is she up to here in Cleveland?

3. Can she be trusted?

"I've heard of the woman you're talking about, she's been out in the field for a number of years now. You could say she's in the same line of work that I am."

"What is she up to?"

"All I know is that some people got ripped off in Los Angeles, something to do with a certain book that held some pretty incriminating stuff and they want it back."

" Trust her? Reggie asked, about as much as you trust anyone, but yes from what I heard about her you can. "One thing, Ruben, she kills pretty easily and she's good at what she does."

"Is she as good as you Reggie?"

"No! But then, one never knows."

Meanwhile, Willow was engaged in a call with Mr. Bosta.

"I didn't wake you, did I? Janice, what news do you have for me, do you have my book?"

"Soon, Mr. Bosta. I'm getting close. The four people are now down to three. Do you want to hear about it?"

"No, not really, Janice. All I want is my book. I must have that book. Are you still in Alaska?"

"No, sir. I'm in Cleveland, Ohio now. These guys move around a lot."

"One thing has come up since I last talked to you; they contacted me and it looks like they went through the book and guess what? Now, they want money for its return—a lot of money. I don't think they figured it out yet but there's always a chance they will."

"I've got help here, so it may make it easier to find them. They know this area very well so I'm hoping this will help."

"Any bites yet, Janice?"

"You might say they found me and where I'm staying. I had just got into town, that shouldn't have happen. They sent one of theirs after me but he won't be going back to them."

"Janice, if you locate that book for me, I'll give you 1% of what they're asking, excluding the fee I'm paying you already."

"Sounds good to me, Mr. Bosta, because I am running into some unexpected expenses."

"Don't you worry about money, Janice. Just concentrate on that book."

6

THE LADY'S CLUB

BEFORE RUBEN HUNG up with Raymond, he found out who the guy and his wife he was supposed to tail were. He thought he'd look into them at the same time he was doing that job for Janice. A kind of a two for one deal. She doesn't need to know about it.

Jimmy Novak and his wife, Bella, live on the west side of town near the lake in a two-story home, with a boat landing leading out to the water. They have two new cars, and a curved driveway. Jimmy was into the clothing industry and his wife was just icing on the cake. I guess old boy was getting tired of it. He told Raymond he felt something just wasn't right, you

know how you just have that feeling? Plus, he needed a change. He's been with her over five years now and she spends money like a water fountain pours water. I'm not knowing where the money goes he says. Four nights a week she goes out with the girls, she says. There is a group of them that hangout together, all around the same ages. His wife is 38 years old, and all her friends are married to well to-do men. And they all belong to at least two social clubs and a charity or two. I took down their addresses and the clubs they belong to and thought I'd start there.

Lake Erie hotel

Basil, the leader of the group that ripped Bosta off in

L.A. ,was in a discussion with the others. Carl had been missing for over 24 hours and should have checked in by now.

He was sent to take care of the woman, who has been bird-dogging them since they made that heist in L.A...

She got close to them in Alaska, or you might say they almost got close to her. She got lucky, with a little help. After receiving word that she followed them to Cleveland and where she was staying, Carl was sent over to take care of her for good. However, he hasn't showed up or even called since then.

"It don't look good. I hate to say this, Levi, but the girl got to him and I'll have to tell you that couldn't have been easy. Carl knew his business."

"What about another try at her?" Alex said.

"I think she probably moved by now. How in the hell does she keep locating us like this? I'll tell you what I think, the book is the key. Since we contacted the owners, we know they're willing to give up big bucks for it. I think I'll try one other thing to get that

bitch off our ass."

"We gonna let her get away with killing Carl? We shouldn't do that," Levi said.

"It's just business, Levi, but you're right. Regardless of how this turned out, we have to take her out."

"How much did you ask for the book?"

"Well, I was going to ask for 100,000 but after I found out why they really wanted that book, I decided to ask for 250,000. Just to see, to throw it out there. You know?"

"So, you asked for 250,000?"

"Yeah, that's what I asked for this time. If they pay that, I'm sure they'll pay more. Do you have any idea what's in the book, Levi?"

"No, I don't, it's in code. But, I'm beginning to get an idea, but to be sure, I'm going to call in someone who could tell us for sure. If it's that important to them, then the sky is the limit."

"Are we going to search for Carl?"

"No, he'll show up eventually, if he's alive."

"Ruben, there is a Miss Janice Willow on line one."

"Hey Janice, what's up?"

"Ruben, I just wanted to let you know I changed hotels. I'm at the Bishop resorts, room 626. Do you know where it is?"

"No, but I can find it. You decided to change hotels?"

"I thought it would be best, don't want to give them another shot at me, so to speak. You making any headway so far?"

"Not yet, Janice. As you know, I only just started. Give me a chance to make a few phone calls and let's get together tonight and do the club thing. I'm sure these guys go out."

"You never said if you knew what they look like or

not. Could you recognize them if you saw them again?"

"I didn't recognize the one in the room, but there is one from Alaska. Once we locate him, I'm sure we can find the other two. I talked to my client and he said they have been in contact with him and they're talking about an exchange for the book."

"How much?" Ruben asked.

"$250,000," Janice replied. That must be one hell of a book. Is your client willing to pay that kind of money?"

"If we don't get to the book first he will."

"You know, Ruben, if we can't locate the book before the transfer is made, maybe we could make the transfer and get to them that way."

"That's a thought. It'll be a couple of days, and my client needs time to get that kind of money together."

After lunch, Ruben decided to find where the Novak's lived; off the lake on Stone Drive, in a two-story home on the upper east side of the lake. There was a three-car garage and a flagpole out front with a U.S. flag on it. A late model car sat in the driveway. I drove by twice and then headed to the social clubs. I was told that the wife, Bella, was 5 foot 2, and one hundred and five pounds, with a small frame and red hair. She wasn't very cute but to each his own. She must have something but what do I know? That ain't my business. He likes it or liked it, I guess the honeymoon is over.

7

THE MEDUSA COMES OUT

JANICE WOKE UP at 1:15 a.m., sat up in bed, wide awake. Then, "it" came out. The hairs on the back of her neck were standing up and her fingers seem to be extending longer than normal. Her fingernails were curling, her face was growing hair, and her teeth were growing outside of her mouth. The lips that were once curvy, lavish, and warm were now curved up into a Dr. Jekyll grin. The legs that were once smooth, long, and toned, were now short, stubby, and hairy. She felt the need to hurt or kill someone—man, woman, or kid. Black or white—there was no discrimination in what she did. She put on her clothes—a black shirt, shoes, pants and hat—and walked out onto the patio door and down to the boardwalk.

She didn't stay there but went underneath, looking up at the bottom, and eventually saw a

drunk stumbling to his sailboat.

He reached the boat and started climbing the stairs, then fell back down, got up and started back up again. Once he was on the boat, he collapsed on the deck and laid there passed out. Janice climbed onto the boardwalk and when she reached the boat, she looked over the railing and climbed on board. The drunk was a 58-year-old traveler—a single, white male. He didn't have any kids but there were kids everywhere—he used to call himself a player back in the day. He travelled the world on his boat with no worries or attachments. He was a free spirit, and that's how he died.

Janice pulled out her Japanese throwing knife and cut his throat from ear to ear, then looked at him for a few minutes and thought, *Too easy, just too easy.* She left the way she came.

The next morning, she looked out her patio door and spotted ten to twelve police officers with crime scene tape all around a sailboat about a half-mile down the boardwalk. They were taking a body off a boat and putting it into a van. The waiter came by with her breakfast and she asked him what had happened. He informed her that someone had gotten murdered the night before and that's all he knew.

"Is there anything I should be worried about?" Janice asked. "After all, I picked this arena because it was said to be quiet and peaceful."

The waiter remarked, "This is the first time anything like this has happened." Janice thanked him, gave him a tip, and finished eating her food.

I try, I really do, Janice thought. But ever since I was a little kid, I've had this thing about killing.

Every so often, I would wake up in the middle of the night and have the urge to kill somebody—anybody.

I've killed my kittens, puppies and birds when I was a kid. I also killed my kindergarten friend, my teacher, my father and aunt, a kid I met at homecoming on spring break, a cop that I had an affair with when I was only 15, and a kid in the park who tried to molest me. There was actually two of them. I killed one and would have kill the other but he got away. I also killed an insurance investigator and a couple of people that happened to be there in the park. I killed all these people before I finished high school.

I tried to tell my mother and father but no one would listen—they never listened. My uncle knew and tried to tell them that I needed help but again, they wouldn't listen. Before my parents passed away they had asked him to take me in and look after me, but he knew better. He told them he would but then after they passed, he told me, no way! So, we worked out a deal

so that I would stay in my parents' house until I

graduated high school

and then went my separate way. Worked out
pretty well too.

The thing about those killings is that I have had no
remorse; never have and I guess I never will.

The Medusa I have tattooed on my butt is very
fitting. It's very telling, if one would only look.
Sometimes, she felt like and looked like Medusa.
That's when "it" came out and she just had to kill
somebody—anybody.

"Janice, you have found a nice place over here. I heard of this area but I never stopped by; it's quite nice."

"Yes, I've always liked being near the water. I may even buy a boat when I retire."

"When I was coming in from the parking lot, one of the attendants told me of a murder here last night."

"Yes, I heard about that. It happened about half a mile from here. If you look out my patio door, you can still see the crime scene tape. They've been there most of the day."

"Well, I know it wouldn't shake you up. So, I won't worry about it."

"Has anything come up about the book I should know about?"

"The people that have the book have gotten in

touch with my client demanding money. He thinks they may have found out what's in it, or at least know its valuc."

"My client is willing to pay using us as an intermediary."

"When is this supposed to take place, Janice?"

"Within the next few days. They will call and let me know where to call them to set up a meeting to decide where the exchange will take place."

"How do we know that the book hasn't been copied?"

"We don't. Mr. Basta just has to take his chances. If they do something like that then, that'll be another story and I'll deal with it."

"You know, they're probably not feeling too good about you, as far as taking out one of their people. They may be thinking about getting back at you."

"I know, and that's been at the back of my mind. I don't want you to worry about it. I'll handle it. For now, just get me over to the meeting place and to wherever else I need to go in town."

"I hope we're not going to need any more clean up," Ruben spouted out.

"You never know, that'll depend on them."

The Ebony Lounge was an out of the way place where lovers go to have a quiet rendezvous. It was nice and quiet and convenient, where you could also talk without big ears listening. Ruben picked it and assumed the other side checked it out before they gave their okay. Besides them checking it out, Janice also wanted to check it out herself.

She told Ruben, "Nothing against you, I just always like to protect my own ass." The lounge had an entrance way and a side door. The foyer, as you walked in, had a reception desk, and leading into the lounge was a thirty-foot bar.

There were smaller tables for two or four patrons. The lights were low and in some areas, there were nothing but candles. Ruben and Janice arrived at the spot early so they could get a seat in the back with their backs against the wall. They informed the maître d' that they were expecting someone and to send him to the back.

At 10:30 p.m., the maître d' came back to the table, followed by a gentleman of medium-size, kind of stocky, wearing a dark blue suit with a vest and fedora. When the maître d' left, Ruben stood up and introduced himself. The guest introduced himself as Mr. Basil. Janice said nothing.

"Why don't we get straight to it? Do you have the book?"

"I do," he said.

"Are you prepared to pay? Do you have the money?"

"I think you spoke to my client and he informed you he would use Mr. Kane and myself to handle it, just as soon as we have proof that you have the book. When can we see it?

And what assurance do we get that you haven't made copies?"

"You can see it before you hand over the money, and as far as making copies, there are none and you only have my word for that. Do you have the money?"

"It should be arriving in a few days. If you want cash, and I assume you do, it'll take that long to get here. I will call you when it arrives."

Basil was about to leave when he said, "Miss Willow, you wouldn't happen to know the whereabouts of one of my men, would you? His name is Carl, and he's gone missing."

"Why would you ask me such a thing, Mr. Basil,? How would I know where he is? I've never met the man. But I'm sure wherever he is, he deserves to be there."

"If I didn't know before, I know now. After this transaction is over, he's going to try and off you."

"I'll bet it's when the money changes hands. He may try to keep the money and the book."

"Well, have you thought about this, Ruben? That they'll try to knock you off first? They might think you're my bodyguard."

"No, not really, Janice. So, what do you have in mind? I think a contingency plan is in order. There are three of them and two of us."

"I don't think they know that we know. We need to cut those odds down. I hope they are not thinking Carl is coming back."

"No, you made it pretty clear that Carl is never coming back."

Basil returned to the hotel to inform the other two what took place at the meeting.

"The money should be here in a day or two, then we will make the exchange and depending on how it goes, we may off the girl and take the money and keep the book.

Carl won't be coming back. She basically confirmed it, so first chance we get, she's dead meat. She has someone with her, so we may have to off him too but first, the money."

Ruben followed Mrs. Novak back to the Elmendorf Hotel where she met a tall, slender guy, about 28 years old. He was nicely dressed in a sports outfit, with a sweater, a button-down silk shirt, and gabardine pants. He had black, curly hair that hung down over his forehead.

She walked up to him and they greeted each other by holding hands and then walked towards the elevator.

I stood and watched it go up to the 9th floor and

stop. Since they were the only ones on board, I knew

that was their stop.

I sat in the lobby with the daily newspaper and proceeded to wait. Two hours and thirty minutes later, Mrs. Novak came back down and had her car brought around front and left.

I decided that instead of following her, I would hang around to try and find out a little more about the fellow she met. Thirty minutes later, he came back down wearing a new outfit. I almost didn't recognize him. He wore a beige suit and shoes, and a silk red shirt that was open at the collar. He walked over to the desk and spoke to the clerk. The clerk reached into a message box and retrieved a note. He walked over to the side and read it, and then tore it up and dropped it in the waste basket. At that moment, an older lady of about fifty-two, who was well-dressed in high heels and a business-type suit walked through the front door. She headed straight over to my boy and gave him a hug. She put her arms around his neck and a light kiss on the cheek. They said a few words to each other and walked towards the elevator and the 9th floor. I headed toward the wastebasket. The three parts of the note said: TB, sorry I won't be able to make our appointment. I hope you'll be available next week. JT.

Well I'll be damned, it seems to me that TB, whoever that is, is for hire. A damn gigolo! Now, that's three women that I know of for sure. I wonder how many others are there. I needed to find out who TB was, so I waited until the desk had a few guests to take care of and walked up behind them and glanced over their shoulder at the message boxes. The boxes didn't have any names on them but had the initials and room numbers. TB's was room number 927.

"Raymond, what do you know about a dude with the initials TB that lives at the Elmendorf Hotel? He's a tall, white guy, is good-looking, and dresses well."

"The only one that comes to mind is a fellow named Teddy Baxter. He's been playing the older ladies since he was 16, and I hear his math teacher got him into it. Apparently, he gave it to her so good that she wanted her friends to get a taste. Teddy's been hitting it ever since, and I hear that's the only gig he ever had. I hear the ladies pay very well—they are all well to-to, or at least their husbands are."

"I noticed that a lot of his business comes to the hotel, and he never got busted."

"Hell no, the hotel gets a cut, plus the ladies get together and pay his rent."

"You know, RK, I would have never thought of Mrs. Novak getting it from old Teddy. I would have thought she had more class than that. Who else is he banging?"

"You only asked me to find out about Mrs. Novak; no one else. If you're willing to pay me, then I'd be glad to give you the names of the others." Of course, he didn't have them.

"By the way, RK, Teddy doesn't live at the Elmendorf, he just conducts his business there."

"Thanks, Raymond."

"Well, your job is done, RK." All he wanted to know was if she was really out there like he figured.

"There is something else here! Sounds like she has Teddy on retainer."

"I don't think he can get a divorce with that, Raymond. I'm gonna have to dig a little deeper. I'll let you know what I come up with."

Willow received a call from a person she had contacted just before the meeting with Basil at the Ebony Lounge. His job was to follow him after he left and find out where he was staying. She never told Ruben—she likes to keep some things to herself—and it's not good for your associates to know too much of your business. If things don't go as planned, then it'll be good to know where she can get a hold of Mr. Basil and the book.

There's just one other thing she asked the contact to do...

"Ruben, this is Don. I got that information you

asked for and you won't believe this; I followed the

Novak woman to the Isabel Social Club and she met

up with 4 other women. They went into a conference

room—it was more like a lounge, with two rooms,

baths, a couple of couches, lounge chairs and a bar.

Things like that. There was a janitor's closet next door

and I was able to slip into it. I hooked up my listening

devices and left. I returned later that night and

retrieve my equipment and went back to my place and

listened to the tape to see what I had captured.

You want to hear it or you want the tape?"

"Both," Ruben said.

"First, they talked girl talk—shopping, hair stuff, latest gossip, where they may go on vacation this year, etc. Then, Teddy came into the conversation. 'You know, Teddy is getting better and better all the time. He must be learning new tricks from somewhere.' 'Oh, honey, I know it's not the one where he kisses you behind the knees, he learned that one from me.' 'Has he done the one with his feet on you—that's really divine. He could do that the whole two hours we're together.' Those were just some of the comments going around. Then, Mrs. Novak asked if everyone was happy with the services Teddy was rendering and asked if they would like to vote on a raise for him. All the ladies agreed. Then, one interjected, saying, 'I think we should double his pay; I've never had a lover like Teddy.'

'Now, now ladies. We don't want to spoil Mr.

Teddy.'

'You don't think we're working him too hard?' someone else commented.

'He's young,' Joyce said. 'He can handle it.'

'Is there any other business before we close?' Mrs. Novak asked. '

'There's just one other thing,' another lady said. 'Is there any chance we could switch days? Someone would like my Tuesday afternoon,' suggested Barbara. Joyce, I would like your Friday morning.'

'That's my only free time, but what about May's Sunday afternoon?'

'I'll switch with you, Barbara,' May said. 'I think that may work for me. Sunday for Tuesday sounds good.'

'Okay then, that settles it. Is everyone satisfied with the two hours' time limit Teddy has given us?'

Everyone was more than satisfied.

'Then, we'll adjourn this meeting for another two weeks.'

There is more, so when you get the tape, you can listen to the rest yourself, but that's the gist of it.

That Teddy must be some kind of a man; I get two nuts and I'm finished for the night. He must be one of those sex addicts I've been hearing about."

"Thanks Don. Send me the tape and your bill. By the way, did you get the names of the other women?"

"No, I didn't, Ruben, but I can. The names I do have are on the tape, and you know the club they belong to."

"I'll tell you what, Don. Get me a picture of the ladies. I already know what the Novak lady looks like and one other. Put their bios on the back of their pictures."

"You got it, Ruben!"

"Ruben, I just received the money from my client and am about ready to set up the meeting with Basil. I need you to be in the background protecting my rear, do you have a weapon?" Willow asked.

"Yes, I do. Do you know when and where the meeting will be?"

"Not yet, but I'll suggest the park; that's always a good location."

The night before the meeting, Basil, Alex and Levi were in the Raimondo lounge having dinner and drinks, celebrating their upcoming windfall.

Alex was saying, "I think I'm going to take a little time off with my share and maybe go up to Canada."

"You've been talking about that for years, and we always head for the next mark. You're just dreaming."

"Our share will be more since we lost Carl. Let's consider taking that money right now; no sense beating around the bush. If we're going to fuck 'em, let's fuck 'em good. In the park, there is an area near the meeting place one of you can hide. When the

money changes hands, you come out blasting.

No talking or haggling or anything like that. The

woman is too dangerous to give her any kind of a chance. She has to go immediately. What about the guy with her?" Alex asked

"He has to go also. So, are we clear about what to do tomorrow night?"

When Basil and his associates headed out for dinner earlier, Willow's contact was watching and called her. She entered their apartment forty-five minutes after they started eating. It took her two minutes to enter their place and then another fifteen to find the book. After another forty-five minutes, she was back in her hotel room packing up. Two hours later, she was on the midnight special to Chicago.

Ruben had gotten a call from Willow the next day saying she no longer needed his services and a check would be sent to him.

"Rita, is that all she said? Nothing else? That's all, RK. Oh yeah, she did say 'thank you'."

What the hell just happened? Ruben thought to himself. One minute, all was set for the exchange tonight, and then, 'Thanks for everything, Ruben. I no longer need your services.' What gives!

I had it all planned and knew what my part in the exchange would be. I had oiled and cleaned my old hammer—my 38—and everything. So, what changed? Janice wouldn't leave without that book. I'm sure of that.

Somehow, she got her hands on it and never told me and skipped town. Well, good for her. Now, I won't have to put my ass out there and get it blown off. If she really ripped off Basil and his boys, they're gonna be mad. Of course, they could have made the exchange without me but then why skip town without saying good bye? No, she ripped them off! She'll really has to

watch her back now.

Willow reached Chicago and hopped on a plane to Los Angeles, and met up with her client who was more than happy to receive his book and the money. He gave Willow 10% and a hefty bonus, and as he put it, was very, very pleased with her services.

Willow spent a couple of nights in L.A. and then headed for Vegas, where what happens in Vegas, stays in Vegas.

Intentionally left Blank

Eddie J Martin

8

TEDDY IN HOSPITAL

THE NEWS TRAVELED fast. Dee called Joyce, who called May and Barbara. Mrs. Novak asked, "What hospital is he in? I don't think we all should go down there together, that would cause a stir. Maybe just one of us should go and inform the others." The just learned that Teddy Baxter was admitted in the local hospital after being attacked the night before.

The perpetrators broke his nose, cracked three ribs

and his knee. In addition, his jaw was broken and

his eyes

were black. The car windows were all broken and set on fire. They were told he'd be laid up for at least six months and was in a coma.

There was a note left in his pocket saying he should get in another line of work. When Mrs. Novak saw him, he was being feed thru a tube and wrapped up from head to toe. Mrs. Novak told the ladies what she saw and all of them shed some tears.

"Do you think, we caused it, May? Maybe one of the husbands got wind of what we've been doing and had it done to him."

"Who would do such a thing?" Joyce said.

"Well, there are five spouses," Dee said. "I believe anyone of them would be capable of having it done. We need to find out who did this and retaliate somehow."

"Not against the ones that did this but the one that had it done," Barbara said.

"How do we go about it?" Dee asked. "I think we should start with some kind of a detective, someone to get us this information."

"Any ideas? May asked.

"I may know of someone who knows someone that I went to school with years ago, and I keep in touch with from time to time. Let me check around," Joyce said. "One thing, ladies. What happens when we find out who put poor Teddy in the hospital? That is, if it turns out to be one of our husbands?"

Two weeks later, at the club, a special meeting was being held by the ladies of Teddy Baxter. The subject of the meeting was the hiring of a detective to help find the person or persons who attacked him.

Joyce had brought recommendations to the group and they voted on who they wanted, and they thought it would be the best fit for them as he knew how to

keep his mouth shut. They talked about getting that

same person to maybe teach whoever a

lesson. At 2:30 p.m., the ladies were sitting in their usual places with their drink in their hands. May and Joyce were on the couch with their legs crossed, and Barbara and Dee were sitting at the bar. Mrs. Novak was standing up facing the door and there was a straight-backed chair in the middle of the room, facing the group. The knock came at the door right on time and Mrs. Novak told the person to come in.

"You were expecting me?"

"Yes, come in and close the door." They pointed him to the chair. After he sat down, she said, "Tell us about yourself, Mr. Kane. It's Ruben Kane, is it not?"

"Basil, you won't believe who I just saw here killed Carl and stole our money."

"You've got to be bullshiting me. How did you happen to run into her?"

"I was just walking around the casino and there she was

at the blackjack table. What do you want me to do? I'm for knocking her off right now."

"I'll tell you what, Levi. If you get the chance, make the hit. Otherwise, wait for Alex and me."

"I think I'm going to fuck this bitch up myself. By the time you two get here, it may be done."

"Levi, watch yourself, she's one bad ass bitch."

Two days later, Basil and Alex arrived in Vegas and went to the Trump Hotel and asked for Levi's room. "I'm sorry, sir," the clerk said, "I guess you haven't heard. The person you're inquiring about committed suicide last night. He jumped off the roof of the hotel. We have no idea why he was up there; drunk I guess. They say he reeked of alcohol when they found him."

Basil looked at Alex, "Suicide my ass. We've got to find that bitch; she's a damn menace."

Alex stepped out of the shower, grabbed a towel and started drying himself. He looked in the mirror and wiped the steam off and glanced at himself. He liked what he saw—a fifty-three-year-old white guy, with nice hair that had only started to bald a little. He had a few strands of gray, and his body was still in shape and he was looking good. He a some hair on the chest but some of the ladies liked that. His waist was kind of getting out of control but cutting down on bread and pasta should help that. His dick was a little too small but there's nothing he could do about that at this stage in life. Earlier, he had considered getting one of those implants but gave that thought up because of the pain he would incur. He had thought about killing one of those black dudes and taking their stuff. Now, that would be something you wouldn't see every day. The original black on white. Black dick on a white guy. Now, that's funny. Alex dropped his head to

pick up his toothbrush and when he looked up in the mirror again there was another face—a black face. A beautiful face but a cold face; one that he'd seen before in Alaska and just missed in Cleveland. The killer of Carl and Levi and the person that stole their money. Without turning around and looking her in the eyes, he said to the mirror, "Janice Willow?" She just nodded and then shot him twice in the back of his head.

Ain't that a bitch. I get hired by the husband to find out who the wife is screwing and find out that there is a group of married women who hired this gigolo. Someone beats the hell out of him and the women think it's one of their husbands. The ladies want to find out who caused their handyman harm, so

they hired someone to find this out for them,

unknowingly to them, me—Ruben Kane.

"RK, a Mr. Novak is on line one."

"Thank you, Rita. Ruben Kane here, what can I do for you?"

"I wanted to thank you for what you did for me and I hope you received my check in the mail."

"Yes, I did, Mr. Novak. That was very generous of you."

"I was wondering, Mr. Kane, if you could meet with me and a few associates of mine, say about 9 p.m. tonight at the yacht club?"

"Sure, Mr. Novak, I'll be able to make that."

"Swell. We'll be expecting you. Just check in at the front desk and tell them who you are; they'll bring you to us."

After I hung up with Novak, Rita asked me what that was all about and I told her the whole story.

"RK, how in the world did you get mixed up in something like that?"

"I don't know, Rita, but it pays well."

Five men from forty-eight to sixty-four years of age were the CEOs and top managers in their individual companies. They were all dressed to the nines, with Rolex watches, three-piece suits, and diamond stick pins. The only one I knew was Mr. Novak and he introduced the rest: Mr. J. Walker, CEO of Walker Tool and Dye; Mr. C. General, CEO of General Hardware; Mr. Wayne Wight, Manager of Wayne Products; E. Blackinshere, Owner of Blackinshere and Things; and of course, Mr. Novak, Owner of Novak Clothing.

"If you don't mind, Mr. Kane, I'll do most of the talking for the group. They'll jump in when they want or feel is necessary. Now, Teddy Baxter. It seems like everyone knew about this guy but me. They also knew of the arrangement their wives had with him, and they arc okay with it. It keeps them off their asses and doing what they do."

"You must understand now that the women don't know that they know."

"Now that I think about it, that'll work for me also."

One of the other men chimed in, "It seems like we have a problem now that Mr. Baxter ended up in the hospital. The ladies have gotten riled up and are out for blood—our blood. We got this from a reliable source; they think it was one of us that had it done. None of us did!"

"Anyway," another one said, "they hired someone to find out for sure and if they can prove it was one of us, well! We know what they're capable of, and they surely have enough money to get it done because we gave it to them."

"So, what do you want from me?"

"Find the people that did that to the Baxter boy and let the women know. We need to end this mess and get back to our normalcy. We all have mistresses we have to get back to and this is throwing a wrench in everything."

"How soon do you want this done? And how much are you willing to pay to get you all out of this fix?"

Novak looked around the room at all the men and said, "Name your price!"

By my count, Willow thought there was only one left—the boss, Basil. Now, the trick is to get to him before he gets to her. One good thing is that they didn't go after Ruben. I guess they figured it was no use anyway—he didn't have the money or the book. He didn't know where she went. They did the right thing. Levi would have been alive if he hadn't seen her in the casino and try to take her on by himself. He assured her that night she would fly for killing Carl and taking their money.

"You think you're a tough bitch. We're going to see if you can fly."

"I'm not waiting for Basil and Alex; they just have to come to your funeral."

"Has anyone ever told you that you talk too much?" Willow said.

"Get in the elevator or I'll shoot your black ass right here. Makes no difference to me but I would like to see if you can fly." Levi picked up Willow as she was going up to her room in the casino, put his 45 in her side, with his hat covering it, and told her to please make a move. Willow felt she could have taken the weapon away from him but thought it would go down a lot smoother once they reached the roof. Willow had training in karate and was a 2nd black belt, and felt it would be no problem at all to take him out. If he would have waited for the other two, then it would have been a different story—maybe. It hadn't occurred to her to throw Levi over the roof of the tower, but since he brought it up...

Once they were out of the elevator and on the roof,

Levi kept the weapon in her side as they walked over to the roof's edge. At the edge, Willow let Levi ramble on about why he hated her and what he was about to do to her. Willow told

Levi again, "Didn't I tell you that you shouldn't talk so much?" And at that moment, she made her move and took his gun away, just like that. Levi couldn't believe it. One minute he had the gun in his hand and the next it was in Willow's. "I told you," she said as she turned him around and helped him over the edge. "You talk too much. If you're gonna do, then do."

Levi was so stunned that he didn't even have time to scream on his way down.

Alex was very easy. Finding out what room he was in and opening the door was no problem for her, but catching him in the shower was due to a bit of luck. She just watched him admiring himself in the mirror. He must think he's some kind of a man, she thought. Little did he know he only had minutes to live. Give him a little more time, she thought. Never let it be said that she's heartless. Alex's combed his hair back with his fingers, patted his face with his open palm,

smoothed his moustache

down and fluffed the hairs on his chest. He then patted his midsection and grabbed his penis and shook it up and down once or twice, then shook his head as if to say, "I could have done better." He reached down for his toothbrush and raised his head to the mirror. That's when Willow stepped into view. He saw her pointing what looked like a canon at him and he knew he was a dead man. He never turned around, and still facing the mirror, said, "Janice Willow!" She just nodded and that was the last thing Alex saw; he never heard the shot that killed him. Basil had called Alex from the casino three times. They had made arrangements to meet at the poker table. So, after not reaching him the first two times, he just figured he was on his way down. After waiting another thirty minutes, he decided to call again, then thought, to hell with it and went up to his room. After knocking a few times, a maid walked by and he persuaded her to open the door

for him.

Basil walked in with her following behind him and eventually ended up in the bathroom. There was Alex at the mirror, leaning over with his face in the sink and the back of his head missing. Basil stood where he was in disbelief and said to himself, "Willow." It looks like she's no longer the hunted but the hunter. The maid screamed and ran out of the room.

Basil was back in his room ten minutes later, packing his bags for a flight to Oklahoma. He felt he had taken enough of a loss and was willing to leave it at that. Know when to fold them—that's his motto. That's why he's the boss, or was the boss. There is no one to boss around now. The book was gone, the money was gone and his three men were gone. Those guys were with me for a long time, through thick and thin, you might say, and I'll miss them. But, a leader always knows when to pull up stakes and now is that time. I'm out of here! Maybe later I can regroup and start back again where I left off. As far as Miss Willow is concerned, I'll put a hit out on her as soon as I get settled.

I have to kill her. I owe it to Carl, Levi and Alex and I owe it to myself. I'm gonna get that done, so help me.

Eddie J Martin

9

AND THEN THERE WERE NONE

Eddie J Martin

BASIL HAD CALLED down to the desk to request transportation to the airport. As he was leaving the elevator, he spotted Willow coming toward him from the desk and reaching into her purse. Basil dropped his bag and reached in his inside coat pocket for his weapon and was pulling it out when suddenly, Willow started screaming and saying, "Gun, gun! He has a gun!" Her hand was still in her purse when Basil pulled his out and started firing at her. The two police officers that were on duty in the hotel did not hesitate. They did not ask Basil to drop his gun, and did not give him any type of warning, they just started firing at him. Both officers emptied their Service revolves into him and were reloading before they went up to him. Willow came out of the cubbyhole she had taken refuge in, picked up her overnight bag and went out the front door to a taxi for the airport.

"Raymond, I guess you heard about Teddy, He's down at St. Elizabeth Hospital in a coma. I hear he's going to bc thcrc for a while, if he ever comes out of it."

"Yeah, Ruben I heard, I wonder what the ladies are going to do about replacing him. If they're asking for volunteers, I am available."

"You know about the ladies, Raymond?"

"Sure I do, from old man Novak. Not everything, but I guess he figured that since I found you for him, it was all right I know. Anyway, what do you need, Ruben?"

"I need to find out who messed Teddy up and put him in the ICU."

"The only thing I heard was that old Teddy liked to gamble—horses, poker, numbers—things like that.

Eddie J Martin

It's a wonder where he gets the time but you know if

he got in with the big boys and got behind..."

"You hear what I'm saying?"

"Yeah, I do, Raymond."

"Any ideas?"

"It could be anyone, you know they've got groups like that all over town. But the biggest I'd say is Tricky and his gang. They cover the race track and do a little loansharking. They're all tough boys but tricky would rather bust you up if you owe him than kill you. He believes in not killing the hand that feeds him."

"Thanks, Raymond. I think you may have solved the case for me."

"Which means it's worth something. Is that right, Ruben?"

"Maybe, Raymond. Watch your mail."

"Hey Ruben Kane, can we do anything for you?"

"No thanks, ladies. I don't think so. I can't afford you."

"For you, Ruben, we'll give a discount."

Salt and pepper were two prostitutes who worked the boulevard—one white, one black. They found working together would be more economical and give their clients a choice.

They say they charge a little more but it's worth it. There're known by the new black Thunderbird they drive around in.

Once, I sat at the bar and watched the girls go out back with client after client, and they spent no more than 15 minutes with each of them. They say they'll

retire in 5 years, and I believe 'em!

Eddie J Martin

Tricky was based in a booth in the upper floor of the race track; four other booths surrounded his, with at least two men in each. Two women were in one of those booths who looked like your everyday bimbo, but I'm sure if they were working for Tricky, they knew their shit. To get to Tricky, you had to go through at least one of those booths. I stood in the clubhouse above, drinking a JB and watching what was going on. A few people were going up to Tricky through the booths and talking to him. Now, everybody that tried didn't get through but the ones that did, you would think Tricky was the godfather or something. They would leave with a smile on their face and I see Tricky write on a pad and hand it to them. No cash was ever exchanged.

Since I had no clear plan and the guy had at least eight people around him at any one time, the only thing I knew was to go after him straight ahead—either ask for a loan or get to him another way by asking him straight up if he fucked Teddy up. I don't think he'd like the latter but it would cut to the chase. I don't know what I'd do if he said 'yes'.

It took a few minutes to get past the entourage but I finally did—with a little lie here and there. I found myself in the presence of the man himself, Tricky!

"What is your name and your business with Tricky?" Up close, he looked entirely different. I saw a person of about fifty-two years old, 5 foot 5, 275 pounds. He had a potbelly, a clean head and face. He held a notepad and pen in his right hand and was smiling,

always smiling.

"My name is Ruben Kane. I'm investigating the attack on Teddy Baxter. What can you tell me about that?"

"I know Teddy, he likes to gamble. He even gambled with me a few times, but I don't have any idea who would want to hurt him. When there's money involved, it could have been anyone. I know what you're thinking, Mr. Kane, but it wasn't me. Teddy would never not have payed me if he owed me—you can bet your last dollar on that. I'm sorry about what happened to him. I liked him but, Mr. Kane, you're barking up the wrong tree. Now, Mr. Kane, you've taken up enough of my time, goodbye!"

"One other thing, Mr. Tricky. Any ideas on the direction I should take next?"

"I do not, Mr. Kane, but there are smaller players than me, not as cool as me but they're out there." Then, he wrote something on his notepad and handed it to me. On the paper was a name: Becky Lee.

I thanked him and told him if I ever needed a loan, I'd be sure to make him my first stop. "Don't do that, Mr. Kane." He wasn't smiling when he said it.

That night, I headed for the Ebony Lounge. If you want to get the low-down on somebody, then go there.

Anybody that's anybody can be found at the lounge, or give it time and they'll show up sooner or later.

On the way there, I passed the block where the

kids were harmonizing. I pulled to the side of the

street, took out my half pint of JB from under the seat,

and listened.

Eddie J Martin

There were four young kids between the ages of 13 and 16. You would think it would be kind of late for them to be out at this hour, but parents aren't the same as when I was growing up. My parents would have put a foot up my ass if I stayed out this late. A lot of parents would have gone to jail for child abuse today. What was unusual about this group was that the tallest one was the lead singer and the tenor, and the shortest one—no more than 5 feet, was the bass. It was the damndest thing I ever saw, a little guy with a voice like that. I tried to hit that bass myself and I'm a grown up, and I still couldn't do it. I listened for another 30 minutes or so, sipped my drink and then moved onto the Ebony Lounge.

It was Wednesday night and the joint was jumping. There was a live four-piece band and standing room only. There were several people I knew from off the block and a couple I went to school with.

Several new people were there. I guess they were from the south—you could always tell by the way they dressed. They weren't cool yet, like us northern boys. Just give 'em a few years. A lot of them were moving up north because of the jobs. My family moved up because all the coal mines were closing. I managed to make it up to the bar and order a double JB on the rocks. You never know when I'd be able to order another with all these people in here.

After wandering around the lounge asking questions, I ran into one guy I knew from the block named Sammy. He shined shoes and was pretty good too. But that's not the only thing he does; he's also the lookout for the numbers racket. He's been doing that for years.

Sammy knows a lot and I wanted to know what he knew about Becky Lee and the loansharking business. I started by asking him what number had hit that night and he told me 412.

"I be damned! I missed it again! I've been playing that number for six months and the day I don't play it, up it pops. Life isn't fair, Sammy, it just isn't fair!"

"Damn, RK, it happens. You need a few bills?"

"I damn sure do, Sammy, but what I need is a little more than I think you can handle."

"Hell, try me." I put an amount in his ear and he said, "Yeah, you're right, RK. I can't touch that. But I may be able to tell you where you can get it."

Sammy named off a few guys that deal in money loaning and their interest rates and who he thought would be my best bet.

Becky Lee was one of those lenders. "I don't know about him," I told Sammy. "I hear if you're late or can't pay, he does something bad to you, like that Teddy guy I heard about. Is he still in a coma?"

"Teddy thought Becky was bullshiting when asked for his money, but he gave him chance after chance. Teddy felt that because Becky liked him, he'd let him slide. Well, he got father then a lot of others, but business is business and if people saw Becky letting Teddy off the hook, everyone would try it."

"I don't know if I wanna get a loan from him, Sammy. They sound like some tough old boys."

"Yeah," Sammy said, "especially that Thomas dude. He's one bad mother jumper. The other two just follow his lead and then all of them take their orders from Becky."

"I heard that Teddy dude may croak."

"Oh well," Sammy said...

You have to give it to them, the guys on the block are all heart.

"Rita, any messages?"

"Your wife called, RK, to remind you to pay the water bill. You also received two checks, one from Mr. Novak and the other from that Willow woman. Both are of substantial amounts."

In the next week or so, we should receive a couple more if things work out. You may have a nice raise in there somewhere."

"Hot damn! Oh, and Alice called, she wanted to know if you were ever going to call her. She's tired of calling you. Bernie called also and said you hit on your number last night but since they're into you for so much now, they'll just take it out of what you owe them. That's about it, RK. You're not coming in today?"

"No, I don't think so, Rita. I've got a few things to do out here. I'll see you tomorrow."

"I hope you don't have to make any more phone calls, Ruben. When you said we were going to spend the day in bed, I didn't know you were going to be on the phone all morning."

The young lady that was complaining was named Ida. I met her for the first time right after talking to Sammy. A little honey of about 5 foot one and 105 pounds. She was so small I thought I could put her in the palm of my hand, but looks can be deceiving.

We left the Ebony Lounge at about 1:30 a.m. and got into my ride. First, I noticed I was just about out of gas and almost didn't make it to her apartment. The girl was looking so good at that point that I was willing to get out and walk. I had to call Rita, and this will make you laugh! I was so high when I came in with the girl, I don't even remember having sex with her. So, you see I had to have makeup time, and it may take the rest of the day.

I left Ida's place at seven that night and proceeded to Skippy's diner. Man can't live on sex alone, got to be some meat and potatoes in there somewhere.

Before I did that, I stopped by the nearest service station and got a shock. Gas had raised to $.22 a gallon up from 18. What the hell is this country coming to? The attendant said, "I've been told in the near future, it's going to get as high as $.42 a gallon." I'll start walking when that happens.

10

THE BATS WIN

I DON'T KNOW where they picked me up, it was either at the service station or Skippy's diner. I had made a few stops after that and then headed for the warehouse district.

They pulled in front of my Buick, and the three of them jumped out of their four-door Packard. One held a forty-five automatic and the other two held baseball bats. I closed my window and locked my doors.

They banged on my hood with their bats and broke my driver's side window, and the guy with the forty-five came up to me and warned me to mind my own business or I'd get what Teddy got. "Do you understand?" I assured them I did. One of the guys added, "I don't think he does, let's pull his ass out of there." As they were about to bust in and pull me out, there came a police siren. They looked up towards the sound and the one with the forty-five pointed it at me, shook it and said to me, "Next time." They left in a hurry and two minutes later, the cops came and passed right by me; they were going on another call. Well, looks like I'll be walking for a few days. One window was broken, there were dings on my hood, and I believe one of them even kicked my door in. If I had doubts before, I know now that Becky and his boys are the ones that did Teddy in and if I don't watch out, they'll be doing me. This is cause for a drink. I reached under my seat and brought out my half pint of JB, of which I only had one small corner left, but it sure was good.

I dropped off my Buick the next morning at the repair shop and headed for the office, Rita was sitting at her desk painting her nails, then saw me and said something like, "Look what the cat dragged in! Good morning, RK!"

"Is the coffee ready, Rita?"

"Be right there, RK."

I threw my hat on the hat rack and pulled off my coat and hung it up. I sat down at my desk, pulled out my bottle of JB and waited for my coffee. After Rita left, I poured a nice hit into my coffee and sat back and relaxed. Five minutes later, I started going through my mail, and looked through my checks first. I smiled when I saw the denominations. I kept going through my bills until I ran across the water bill for my apartment. I'll be damned! I was two months behind.

"RK, Mrs. Novak's on line one. She sounds pretty upset."

"Good morning, Mrs. Novak, how can I help

you? I'm still working on your case and making some progress."

"That's great, Mr. Kane, but I didn't call you specifically for that. I wanted to tell you that Teddy passed away last night. Now, it's murder and we— the ladies—want his killer worse than ever."

"I'm very sorry for your loss, Mrs. Novak, and please express my feelings to the other ladies. I guess you want me to drop the case and let the police handle it now?"

"By no means, Mr. Kane. Continue what you are doing and we'll pay you twice what we offered you— we want them. If the police find them first, great. All right, Mrs. Novak, I'll stay on it."

I'm damn sorry for Teddy but things aren't looking too good for me either. I think Becky's boys know I suspect them and may have turned the cops onto them. So, if I were them, what would I do? Knock off one Ruben Kane, that's what I'd do.

Maybe to save myself a lot of grief, I should call Lieut. Jeffries down at the Cleveland Police Department. Jeffries and I had worked a few cases together. In fact, I helped him so much with one case that he got a promotion because of it. So, he's always open to what I have to say—somewhat.

He's crazy about me.

"Lieut. Jeffries, how you doing, buddy? I haven't seen you in a while."

"Kane, what the hell you want? I'm a busy man

and don't have time for your BS. So, make it quick."

"Now, is that any way to talk to the guy that got you that lieutenant's bar. Damn, seems like I could get just a little more respect. How soon we forget."

"All right, all right, Kane, you made your point. Now, what the hell do you want?"

"The Teddy Baxter case, are you familiar with it? He's the guy that got beat up pretty good off 79th and Cedar. Was in a coma?"

"Yeah, I may have heard something about that but you know I'm a Lieutenant now and small crimes like those don't get to my desk."

"Well, what about murder; would murder do it?"

"That would do it, Kane."

"Well, Teddy Baxter just died last night, he never regained consciousness."

"I take it you know something about his death?"

"I may know a little something," and I went on to tell him how I got involved and who hired me and the attack Becky's boys put on me the night before. I also told him what they said about getting me like Teddy.

"Okay, Kane, thanks. We'll look into it."

I hope those old boys don't blame me for dropping a nickel on them. They're not too far off my ass now.

Mr. Novak called not long after I talked to Lieut. Jeffries.

"Mr. Kane, have you heard about Teddy Baxter yet?"

"Yes, I have, Mr. Novak. I was sorry to hear that, but I guess your troubles are over for you and your associates."

"No, no, they're not, Mr. Kane. We didn't want this. With Teddy alive, he kept our wives out of our hair and we could do what we wanted."

"What about the divorce you wanted? Did you change your mind about that?"

"Yeah, I did. The others convinced me it was cheaper to keep her. You have to find out who killed Teddy now, they'll always believe it was us. How close are you to finding that out?" he said.

"I'm about to wrap it up," I lied.

"You do that, Mr. Kane, and you'll always have five grateful men in your debt."

"I'll hold you to that, Mr. Novak."

Outside the office I

was debating between whether to take a cab or streetcar to go to lunch. Since I've ridden enough streetcars in my life, I decided on the cab. Skippy's place was for lunch but since it was between lunch and dinner, and they never change menus anyway... Small steak and potato, salad, roll and iced tea.

After dinner, I thought I'd give Alice a call and an hour later, I was walking through her front door. I felt that if I stayed out of sight for a while, it would give the police the opportunity to pick up Becky and his boys. I would take the credit, get paid and all would end well. I laid up with Alice all night until ten the next night and told her I had to get to work. I really needed a drink and wanted to go to the Cave Club. I should have stayed at Alice's a couple more days because once I got out of the cab, two of Becky's boys grabbed me. The one that seemed to love his forty-five so much stuck it in my back and walked me to the alley. Halfway down,

the Packard was parked. Becky let the window

Down.

"Mr. Kane, you've been putting your nose where it shouldn't be and that's in my business, you shouldn't do that. My business is my business. Thomas gave you a warning, but I see you don't take to warnings. So…" Then he raised his window and drove away. Thomas, the one with the forty-five, moved back and one of the old boys with the baseball bat came at me and swung like he was looking for a home run using my head. I ducked and moved back towards the center of the alley. The other one, same type of bat (they must have had a sale on bats) came at me from the other side and wrapped me on the shoulder. I really felt that one. The first guy came at me again and caught me in my right side, then the other one came at my leg and took me to the ground. Then, they went to work on me with Thomas, and his forty-five looking on. My head, elbow, ribs and hips. I think one guy even hit me on

the sole of my feet. I was able to get one good

punch at one of them, and I hit him in his nuts. Naturally, he came down to the ground with me and I grabbed his bat and hit the other guy with a bat in his knee, hard. Things weren't going the way Thomas wanted them to, so he pointed his forty-five at me and chambered a round. The next thing I saw were two red spots, right where Thomas' heart was supposed to be. He looked at the spots, fell to his knees and then to the ground with a surprised look on his face. I turned towards the guy I had hit in the nuts and saw he was trying to get up, so I sung the bat as hard as I could toward his head and heard something crack when it connected. The other bat welder was sitting on the ground moaning and holding his knee. I stood up and walked towards him with the bat. He held up his hands to protect his face and said, "No, no, please."

"No, my ass."

His hands didn't help him. After the fourth or fifth

swing, I set back down on the ground breathing

hard and feeling around for any broken bones or if I was hurt otherwise. I heard high heels coming my way down the alley but I was too tired and hurt to move. When the person got to me and stopped, it was then that I took the effort to look up. There was Janice Willow; black high heels, pantsuit and gloves, and one long-ass Beretta in her hands, still smoking.

"You're something else with that bat, Ruben. You ever play pro?"

"Janice, where'd you come from?"

"We can talk about that later, Ruben. Let me help you up." At the street, Willow said, "We better get to your car and get you home."

"No car, and don't ask, it's a long story."

Ruben and Willow entered his office and he headed straight for the couch, moaning all the

while.

As Ruben laid on the couch, Willow helped him off with his coat and started checking him out for broken bones and everything else.

"You want to tell me what that was all about?"

So, Ruben told her the story and then asked her how she happened to be in that alley at that moment.

"I pulled up in a cab right behind you and saw those men abduct you, and decided I'd follow. Once the guy raised his gun towards you, I felt I'd better intervene."

"You know, I wouldn't have minded if you stopped it a little sooner. What are you doing back in Cleveland anyway?"

"I thought about the way I left and had to come back and thank you myself, and maybe take you out to lunch or something."

"Well, that's nice but as you can see, I'm not going anywhere right now."

"Tell me something, Ruben. How many men are left out of the group that killed Teddy?"

"Only one! The boss, Becky Lee."

"Would you know where I could find him? Got to leave, I'll catch up to you a little later."

"Before you leave, would you get my bottle of JB out of my desk drawer?"

Epilogue

BECKY LEE WOKE up and saw the figure of a gorgeous black woman sitting on his side of the bed, near the foot, wearing only a bra and panties. Ordinarily, he'd have someone in there with him but tonight, he was in there alone. "Who are you?" he asked. "Not that I'm complaining, you understand. Did one of the guys send you up? They should have told me you were coming. What's your name?"

"If you had a last wish, what would it be?" At that point, Becky looked at Janice, sat up in bed and asked her, "Just who the fuck are you and who sent you? Since you're not going to answer my question, I guess I better answer yours."

"My name is Janice Willow and I'm a friend of Ruben Kane's."

"Now, why Ruben Kane send me some drawls, after I sent the boys to fuck him up?"

"Trying to make amends, I guess."

"Well, okay. I accept."

"I'm sorry to disappoint you, Mr. Lee, but I'm not here for that."

"I don't get it, if you're not here to give me the drawls and this Kane guy didn't send you or my boys didn't send you, then what the hell are you doing here?"

"It's very simple, Mr. Lee. I've come here to kill you. I've come to send you straight to Hell."

Becky Lee was reaching under his pillow but he never reached the 38 Smith and Wesson he kept there. Willow had plunged her knife into his throat and moved it from side to side, almost decapitating him, and put a smile below his mouth.

And then there were none.

She had anticipated the blood, the gore and the mess—she loved it. Willow took a shower and cleaned up, put on fresh clothes that she had brought in her overnight bag, and walked out of the apartment. At the main entrance, while she was getting into a taxi, one of Becky's men looked at her approvingly and said to the other, "That Becky is one lucky ass, to sleep with something like that. One day my money will be long enough…"

"Fat chance," the other one said.

Three days later, Janice Willow walked into Ruben's office and said, "You're looking better."

"Yeah, it's amazing what a few days of rest will do. What have you been doing these few days?"

"Oh, I've been here and there. Went to the

racetrack, won a few dollars. Caught a baseball and

basketball game."

"Never knew you were into sports."

"There's a lot of things you don't know about me, Ruben. By the way, how did your business turn out?"

"Well, I informed my clients that the men that killed Teddy had been found dead in an alley up town and brought them the newspaper to prove it. A couple days after that, they found Becky Lee in bed with his throat cut. The husbands got off the hook and I got paid. Everybody's happy."

"Well, it looks like I came back at the right time. How about some lunch?"

End

Other books by this author:

Enlisted at 14...A Memoir

Enlisted at 14 and the journey continues

Enlisted at 14... Looking back

Willow... A novel

Willow... One for the team

Willow... And the Medusa

Little Miss Willow... A Short Story

Assassin

Meet Ruben Kane

R.K. {Ruben Kane}

Ruben's bag

Ruben's bad side

Smooth…A Ruben Kane novel

And Then Some

Just a Dream

Ducks in A Row…Short Stories

www.ingramcontent.com/pod-product-compliance
Lightning Source LLC
Chambersburg PA
CBHW070837120626
46556CB00002B/784